THE USBORNE BOOK OF
EASY
CLARINET
TUNES

Caroline R. Hooper

Designed by Joanne Pedley

Illustrated by Adrienne Kern

(Additional illustrations by Peter Dennis)
Photography by Howard Allman

Original music and arrangements by Caroline R. Hooper

Edited by Emma Danes
Series editor: Anthony Marks

An 18th century clarinet

Introduction

This book contains lots of tunes for you to play on your clarinet. The first few are fairly easy, but they gradually get more difficult as you go through the book. Near the end there are some tunes for clarinet and piano, as well as some for two clarinets.

Whenever a new note appears in the music, there will be a fingering diagram to show you how to play it. You can find out more about these diagrams on the opposite page, and on page 46 there is a chart which shows the fingerings for all the notes in the book.

Musical words and signs introduced in the book are also explained in a section called "Music help" on page 46. It reminds you what all the Italian words mean and tells you how to pronounce them. On page 47 there is a list of clarinet music you might want to listen to and an index of all the tunes. There is also lots of information throughout the book about composers and different musical styles, as well as a brief history of the clarinet.

An 18th century clarinet player

About your clarinet

People use clarinets in many different parts of the world for playing all sorts of music, including classical, jazz, blues and folk. In the past, clarinets were usually made of wood, with metal keys. Wood is still popular today, but some clarinets are made of a special kind of hard plastic. This picture shows all the different parts of the clarinet, and you can see the instrument in more detail at the bottom of pages 3 to 7.

Mouthpiece

Ligature

Barrel

Reed

Keys

Top joint

Rod

Pin

Bell

Bottom joint

Clarinets have five sections: the mouthpiece, the barrel, the top joint, the bottom joint and the bell. The keys are attached to the top and bottom joints by metal rods and pins. The reed, which is made from cane (the woody stem of a plant), is held in position on the mouthpiece by the metal ligature.

How to read the fingering diagrams in this book

The pictures on the right show you which keys on your clarinet to press, and which holes to cover, with each finger or thumb.

Every time you learn a new note, there is a fingering diagram to show you which keys or holes to use. In the diagram, there is a circle for each of the holes. If the circle is filled in, you have to cover that hole.

Some of the diagrams also contain numbers. These tell you which keys to press. You can see each key and its number labelled in the pictures on the right.

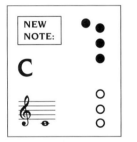

NEW NOTE:

C

The fingering diagram above is for the note C. It tells you to cover the top three holes with the first, second and third fingers of your left hand, and cover the back thumb hole with your left thumb. The bottom three circles are not filled in, so you leave the lowest three holes uncovered.

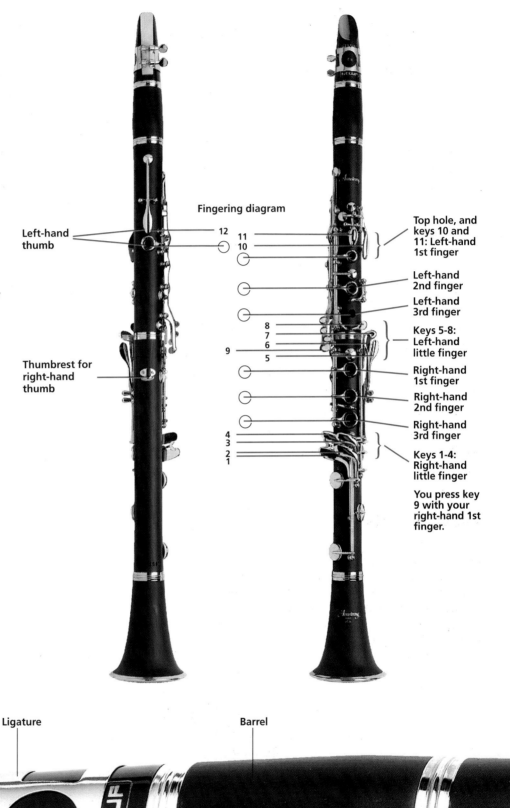

Fingering diagram

Left-hand thumb

Thumbrest for right-hand thumb

Top hole, and keys 10 and 11: Left-hand 1st finger

Left-hand 2nd finger

Left-hand 3rd finger

Keys 5-8: Left-hand little finger

Right-hand 1st finger

Right-hand 2nd finger

Right-hand 3rd finger

Keys 1-4: Right-hand little finger

You press key 9 with your right-hand 1st finger.

Mouthpiece

Ligature

Barrel

Putting your clarinet together

The first thing you need to do is grease the joints. This will make it easier to put the instrument together. You can buy special grease to do this.

Whenever you can, hold the clarinet away from the parts that have keys. If you have to touch the keys, don't press too hard on them.

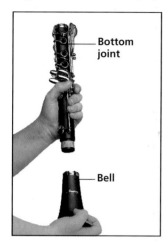

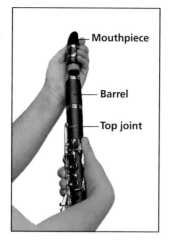

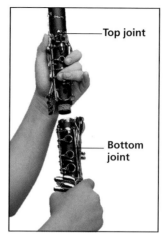

The bell fits onto the widest end of the bottom joint. Hold the bottom joint fairly low down to avoid putting pressure on the keys. Then gently push the bell on.

Next fit the barrel onto the top joint and push the mouthpiece onto the barrel. You might find it easier if you remove the ligature from the mouthpiece before doing this.

Hold the top joint in your left hand. Put your second finger over the middle hole. This moves a small metal lever which makes it easier to fit the bottom joint on without damaging the keys.

Push the two parts together, twisting them very slightly. Don't twist too far in case you knock the side keys against each other. Make sure all the holes are lined up.

Putting the reed onto the mouthpiece

When you have put your clarinet together, fit the reed. Wet it a little in your mouth and place it on the mouthpiece. The flat side should be covering the hole (see right). Try not to touch the tip of the reed when you do this, as it can break very easily.

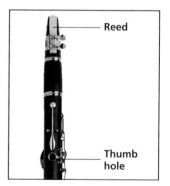

Line up the tip of the reed with the tip of the mouthpiece, then tighten the ligature to hold it in place. Adjust the position of the mouthpiece so that the reed lines up with the thumb hole on the back of your clarinet. Do this by turning the barrel.

How to hold your clarinet

Place your right thumb under the thumbrest. The left-hand thumb covers the hole on the back of the clarinet. You can check which finger covers each hole on the picture at the bottom of pages 4 to 6. Hold the clarinet pointing slightly away from your body (shown on the right).

Making a sound

Rest your upper teeth on the top of the mouthpiece. Cover your bottom teeth slightly with your lower lip so that they are not touching the reed. Put about 1cm (½in) of the mouthpiece in your mouth. Make sure your lips are closed around it so that no air escapes from the sides of your mouth. Place your tongue on the reed, just above your lower lip and say "ta" very gently as you blow. You may find it tricky to make a clear sound at first, but it will get easier with practice.

It might help if you move the corners of your mouth outwards a little as if you are smiling.

Try not to puff your cheeks out when you blow. Always keep your face relaxed.

How to stand

It is always better to stand while playing the clarinet, so that you can breathe freely. Balance your weight evenly on both feet and don't hunch your shoulders. Keep your hands and fingers relaxed and hold your elbows slightly away from your body. If you sit down to play, keep your back straight and don't cross your legs.

Prop your music up at eye level. Do not bend down to read it.

Keep your feet slightly apart, and your weight evenly balanced.

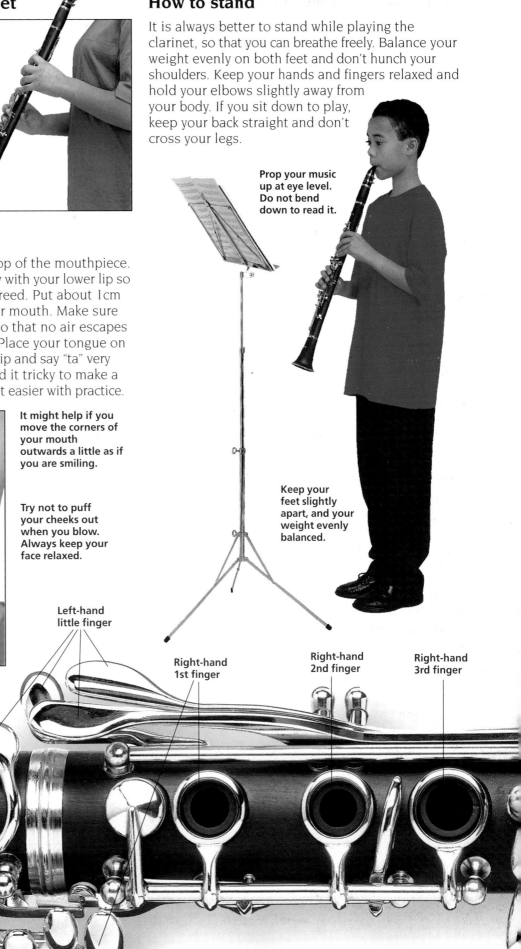

Left-hand little finger

Right-hand 1st finger

Right-hand 2nd finger

Right-hand 3rd finger

Left-hand 2nd finger

Left-hand 3rd finger

Breathing

If you breathe after every note, this will actually make you feel more out of breath. Try to play a few notes, one after the other, without taking a breath. It will also help if you don't puff your cheeks out.

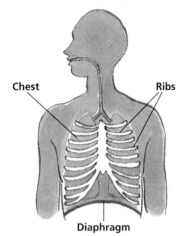

Chest   Ribs

Diaphragm

The best way to play is to take deep breaths, using a muscle in your stomach called your diaphragm ("di-a-fram"). If you put your hand on your tummy and breathe in deeply, you should be able to feel your diaphragm move as it pushes air up into your lungs.

When you are playing, it is important to breathe at the right time. In this book, a comma above the music shows you where to breathe. A comma in brackets shows you an extra place to breathe if you need to. When you take a breath, keep the clarinet still and breathe through the sides of your mouth.

Reading music

Music is made up of notes which are written on a set of five lines called a staff. How high or low a note is is called its pitch. The pitches are named after the first seven letters of the alphabet. You can tell how high or low a pitch is by its position on the staff. A pitch on the top line of the staff is higher than a pitch on the bottom line. You can see the pitches and their names on the staff below.

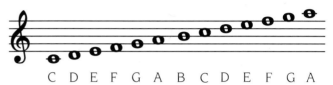

C D E F G A B C D E F G A

Counting

Note lengths are measured in steady counts called beats. On the right you can see three types of note which last for different numbers of beats.

Crotchet = 1 beat	♩
Minim = 2 beats	♩
Semibreve = 4 beats	𝅝

Time signatures

In music, beats are arranged in groups called bars. Numbers called the time signature at the beginning of the music tell you how to count. The top number tells you how many beats are in a bar. The bottom number tells you what sort of beats they are. The number four means they are crotchet beats.

This means there are four crotchet beats in each bar.

This means there are three crotchet beats in each bar.

Clap the rhythm of each tune before you start to play. Make the first beat of every bar slightly stronger than the others.

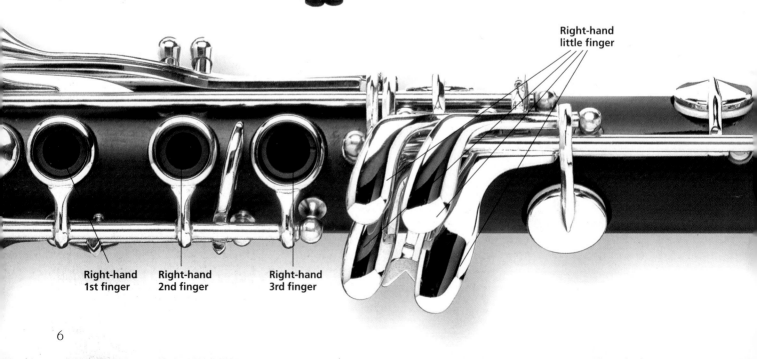

Right-hand little finger

Right-hand 1st finger   Right-hand 2nd finger   Right-hand 3rd finger

New notes

The diagrams on the right show you how to play the notes in the tunes below. Work the fingerings out carefully and try each note before you begin to play the tunes. You can look at the explanation on page three to remind yourself how to read the diagrams. Then look at how each note is written on the staff and practise changing from one note to another several times.

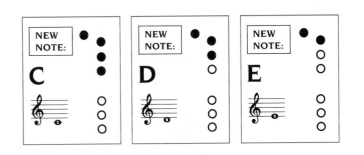

Au clair de la lune

This is an old French tune written by a composer called Jean-Baptiste Lully (1632-1687). The title means "By the light of the moon". It is about a clown called Pierrot. He is writing a letter when his candle is blown out and he has to finish it using the light from the moon.

Little dance

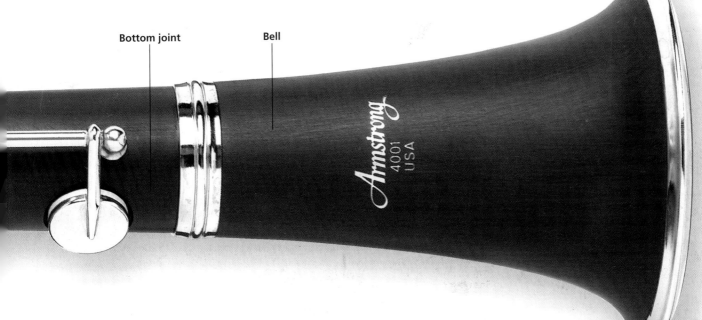

Bottom joint   Bell

Armstrong
4001
USA

Playing G

When you play G, the whole weight of the clarinet rests on your right thumb, as shown in the picture on the right. If you push up with your right thumb, it may help you keep your clarinet steady. This may make your hand feel tired at first, but it will become easier the more you practise. To help you to strengthen the muscles in your hands, try to play for a short amount of time every day. This is better than playing for an hour once a week.

NEW NOTE:

G

NEW NOTE:

F

Ecossaise

An ecossaise is a country dance which was popular in the 19th century. This one was written by a German composer called Carl Maria von Weber (1786-1826).

The dancing duck

This is a lively dance tune, so practise it until you can play it fairly fast. Play it slowly at first, then gradually speed up. Try to play to the end of the first four bars before taking a breath, but you can breathe after two bars if you need to.

15th century musicians playing bagpipes, which were often used to accompany dances

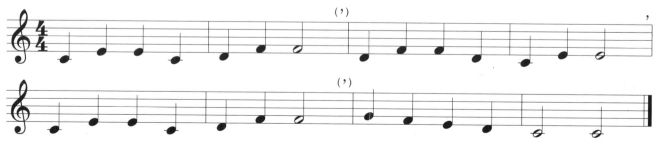

Noël

This is the music for a Christmas song. It was written by a French composer called Louis-Claude Daquin (1694-1772). Make sure you hold all the notes for their full time value, especially the semibreves at the end.

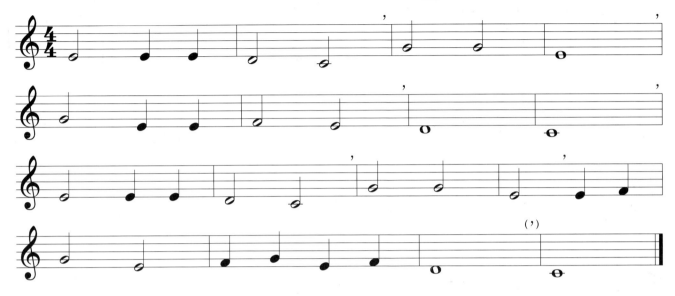

Dotted minims

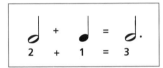

A dot after a note makes it half as long again. A minim lasts for two crotchet beats and half a minim equals one crotchet beat. So a dotted minim lasts for three crotchet beats.

Rag and bone

You have to count very carefully in this piece. It might help to clap the rhythm before you start to play. Remember to count the dotted minims so that they last for three full beats. *Rag and bone* is in a style of music known as ragtime, an early form of jazz that was very popular in the late 19th and early 20th centuries. Try playing the first beat of every bar slightly louder than the others to make the rhythm sound lively.

A band playing ragtime

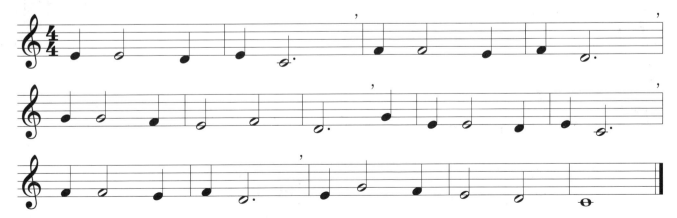

Playing low notes

When you are playing low notes, make sure you keep your head up straight. You may need to blow a little harder for these notes, but don't blow too hard or the sound will be harsh.

Make sure your fingers are covering the holes.

NEW NOTE:

G

Quavers

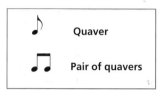

| ♪ | Quaver |
| ♫ | Pair of quavers |

A quaver lasts for half a crotchet beat. Quavers are often joined together in groups of two, three or four.

Clerkenwell green

Ties

Don't play a new note here

Sometimes two notes of the same pitch are linked by a curved line called a tie. When you see this sign, play the first note for as long as both notes added together. Don't play the second note separately.

Ode to joy

This tune was written by a German composer, Ludwig van Beethoven (1770-1827).

Beethoven

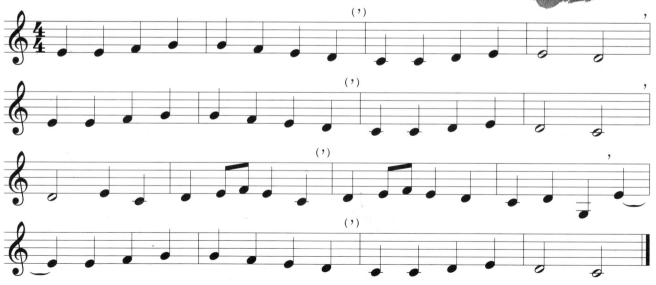

Ländler

This is another tune by Beethoven. It is in the style of an old German dance called a ländler. The ländler was originally a country dance, but by Beethoven's time it was popular in dance halls in many towns and cities.

Upbeats

There are three beats in a bar. The first bar has one beat.

The last bar has two beats.

Sometimes there are notes at the beginning of a piece that do not add up to a full bar. These are called upbeats. It may help to count the missing beats in your head before you start playing. The beats in the first and last bars add up to one complete bar.

Aria

This tune is by Christoph Willibald von Gluck (1714-1787).

Playing hints

Keep your fingers slightly bent, but not too much. Always cover the holes with the pads of your fingers, not the very tips. This helps to make sure the holes are completely covered.

You can check to see if you are covering the holes properly by pressing your fingers down and then removing them. If you can see full circle marks on your fingers, then you are doing it properly.

Playing A

When you play A, keep your fingers close to the holes, but roll your left hand up a little. Press key 11 with the side of your first finger, as shown in the picture.

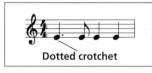

NEW NOTE:

A

Dotted crotchets

Dotted crotchet

Remember, a dot after a note makes it one and a half times its normal length. So a dotted crotchet lasts for one and a half crotchet beats. Clap the rhythm on the left to practise counting dotted crotchets.

Lord Willoughby

This tune was written by an English composer, William Byrd (1543-1623), for a keyboard instrument called a virginal. He liked the sound of the virginal so much that he wrote a whole book of music for it.

A 16th century virginal

Looking after your clarinet

Always clean your clarinet after playing. Use a "pull-through", a cloth with a small weight attached to it by string.

Pull-through

To clean your clarinet, drop the weight down and pull it through the other end. The cloth will follow, cleaning the inside.

You should also wipe all the keys gently with a soft cloth after playing. This will remove any fingerprints.

Dry the pads under the keys by pressing each key down onto a small piece of very thin paper.

Flat signs

This sign is called a flat.

In between the notes named after the letters of the alphabet, there are extra notes called sharps and flats. A flat sign tells you that the note is slightly lower than the letter-name note. So B flat is a little lower than B. Where you see a flat sign, you play any notes that follow in that bar on the same line or space as flats. A flat sign during a piece is called an accidental.

NEW NOTE:

B♭

Aura Lee

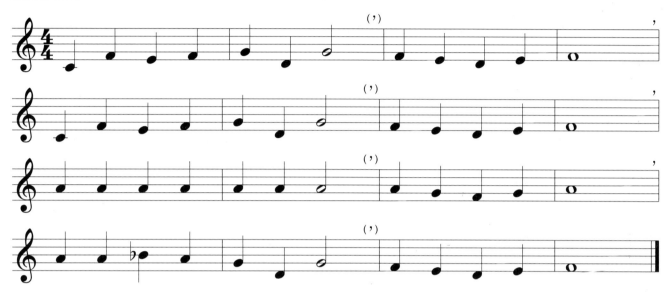

Rests

Crotchet rest (rest for one beat)	𝄽
Minim rest (rest for two beats)	▬
Semibreve rest (rest for four beats)	▬

Sometimes there are silences in music. There are symbols called rests that tell you when there are silences and how long they last for. Three common types of rest are shown on the left. When you see one in a tune, count the correct number of beats in your head before you play the next note.

Plaisir d'amour

This tune was written by a composer called Giovanni Martini (1741-1816). Martini worked at the Paris Conservatoire, a special music school.

The Paris Conservatoire

13

Slurred notes

Tongue the first, third fourth and sixth notes.

A curved line joining two different pitches is called a slur. It tells you to link the notes smoothly. Usually you say "ta" as you play each note, to make it sound clear. This is called tonguing. A slur tells you to tongue the first note, keep blowing, and move your fingers to the next note without tonguing again.

German dance

This tune is by Beethoven.

Beethoven composing at his piano

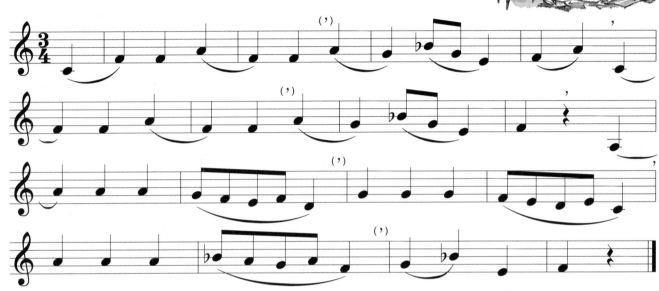

Sharp signs

Sharp sign

A sharp sign makes a note slightly higher. So F sharp is a little higher than F. Where you see a sharp sign, any notes that follow in that bar on the same line or space are also sharp.

NEW NOTE:

F♯

The fox and the hare

14

Repeats

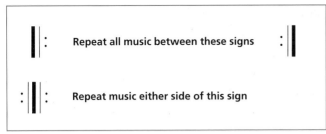

Repeat all music between these signs

Repeat music either side of this sign

Some pieces have sections that you play more than once. They are shown by signs called repeats. The sign with the dots on the right-hand side marks the beginning of a repeated section. If there is no sign like this and you reach a sign with the dots on the left-hand side, go back to the start and play the section again. When you reach the same repeat sign for the second time, ignore it and finish the piece.

Andante

This tune was written by Wolfgang Amadeus Mozart (1756-1791), an Austrian composer. He wrote his first pieces of music when he was only four years old. Repeat the first two lines, then play the second part and repeat that too. *Andante* means "at a walking pace".

Mozart

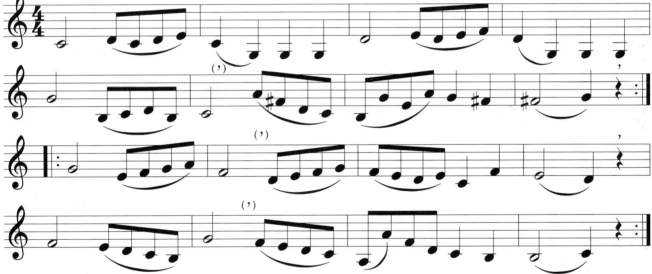

Allegretto

This tune is by Friedrich Berr (1794-1838). *Allegretto* means "fairly fast". The time signature means there are two crotchet beats in each bar.

15

A new time signature

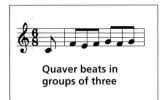

Quaver beats in groups of three

In 6/8 time the beats are counted in quavers rather than crotchets. The number 8 on the bottom of the time signature stands for quavers. The number 6 on the top means that there are 6 quaver beats in each bar. The quavers are divided into two groups of three.

Rondo

This piece was written by an Austrian composer called Ignace Joseph Pleyel (1757-1831). Although his music was very popular in his lifetime, he is now most famous for starting a company that made pianos. Watch out for the slurs.

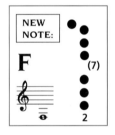

A piano made by Pleyel

The ash grove

For centuries, folk songs were passed on to each new generation without being written down. In the late 19th century, people began to fear that important songs could be forgotten, so they started to write them down. This folk song is from Wales.

Different fingerings

You can play some notes with either a right-hand or a left-hand key. In the diagrams, one key is shown in brackets. When you are learning the tunes in this book, use either all the fingerings with brackets, or all the ones without.

NEW NOTE: **F** (7) 2

Playing loudly and softly

Sometimes there are signs in music to tell you how loudly or quietly to play. These are called dynamics. The letter *f* stands for *forte*, the Italian word for "loud". The letter *p* stands for *piano*, the Italian word for "quiet". The words are Italian because music was first printed in Italy, hundreds of years ago.

More about fingerings

Use the key in brackets for E if you used the bracketed key for F on page 16. This will help you to alternate smoothly between right- and left-hand fingerings in *Tit-Willow*, below.

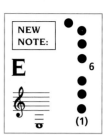

NEW NOTE:

E

6

(1)

Bear dance

Bear dance comes from a set of pieces called *Album for the Young*, a book of piano music for children. This was written by a German composer called Robert Schumann (1810-1856). *Moderato* means "at a moderate speed", not too quickly or too slowly.

Schumann

Tit-Willow

This tune is from an operetta called *The Mikado* by Arthur Sullivan (1842-1900). An operetta is like a play, with singing and dancing. Sullivan wrote many famous operettas with William Gilbert (1836-1911), who wrote the words to the songs. These include *The Pirates of Penzance*, HMS *Pinafore* and *The Yeomen of the Guard*. Remember to play loudly where the music is marked *f* and quietly where it is marked *p*. Take care to make the tied notes the correct length.

A scene from *The Mikado*

Key signatures

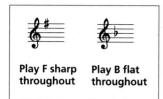

Play F sharp throughout

Play B flat throughout

Sometimes there are sharp or flat signs right at the beginning of a piece, before the time signature. Sharps or flats in this position are called a key signature. The key signature tells you to play certain notes sharp or flat throughout the piece. If there is an F sharp in the key signature, you play every F in the piece as F sharp.

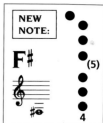

NEW NOTE:

F#

(5)

4

Minuet in G

Johann Sebastian Bach (1685-1750) wrote this tune for his wife, Anna Magdalena. Remember to play F sharp throughout the piece.

Bach's notebook of music for Anna Magdalena

Making a good sound

Each time you practise, start by playing some long, steady notes. Try moving your clarinet a little and tightening or loosening the muscles in your lips. Listen very carefully so you can learn how to make the best sound.

You could also try playing long notes, but getting gradually louder and then quieter. This will help you to control your breathing. Blow a bit harder to get louder, and more gently to get quieter. Always remember to take a deep breath before each note, and let the air out gradually. Try not to let any air escape from the sides of your mouth.

The picture on the right will remind you of some of the things to look out for.

Keep your head up straight.

Don't puff your cheeks out.

Keep your elbows, wrists and fingers relaxed.

Remember not to grip your clarinet too tightly.

Country dance

Play this tune slowly at first, until you are sure of the notes. Then try speeding it up until you can play it fairly quickly. Try to make a contrast between the sections with different dynamics.

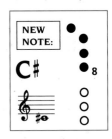

NEW NOTE:

C#

Naturals

The natural sign before the second C cancels out the sharp before the first C.

A natural sign cancels out a sharp or flat on the same line or space earlier in the bar, or in the key signature. Any note on the same line or space after it in the bar without a sharp or flat sign is also a natural.

Little serenade

This tune was written by an Austrian composer called Joseph Haydn (1732-1809).

First- and second-time bars

1.		2.
First-time bar sign		**Second-time bar sign**

Some tunes have two endings. The first time through, play the first-time bar, then repeat the section. The second time through, miss out the first-time bar and play the second-time bar instead.

Mezzo piano and *mezzo forte*

Mezzo piano (often shortened to **mp**) means "fairly quiet", but not as quiet as *piano*. *Mezzo forte* (or **mf**) means "fairly loud", but not as loud as *forte*.

Mistress Campbell's choice

This tune is in the style of a country dance. Watch out for the accidentals. Try playing it slowly at first, then gradually speed it up. *Allegro* means "fast".

Playing E flat

To play E flat, press key 9 with the side of your right-hand first finger.

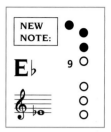

Semiquavers

♪	**Semiquaver**	♬	**Pair of semiquavers**

A semiquaver lasts for half a quaver beat. Groups of two, four or six semiquavers can be joined up.

Arietta

This tune is by Mozart.

Wiegenlied

Wiegenlied is the German word for lullaby. This lullaby is by Mozart. The last bar but one is a bit tricky, so count very carefully to make sure the rhythm is correct.

Dotted crotchet rests

Dotted crotchet rest

Like a dot after a note, a dot after a rest increases its length by half. So a dotted crotchet rest lasts for one and a half crotchet beats.

Gypsy dance

This tune is by Haydn. Make sure you count all the rests carefully and keep the semiquavers steady.

Haydn

Quaver rests

A quaver rest lasts for half a crotchet beat

NEW NOTE:

G♯

3

Playing staccato

Staccato notes

Staccato means "separated". A dot above or below a note tells you to play staccato. Make the note as short as possible. Be sure you keep the speed even, and try not to play staccato notes louder than others. It may help to say "tut" instead of "ta" when you blow.

Getting louder and quieter

Get gradually louder   Get gradually quieter

The sign on the left in the box tells you to get gradually louder. This is called *crescendo*, or *cresc*. The sign on the right in the box tells you to get gradually quieter. This is called *diminuendo*, or *dim*.

Spring song

This tune is by Mozart. He grew up in a very musical family and was taught music from an early age. As children, he and his sister often gave concerts together. *Allegretto* means "fairly fast", but not as fast as *allegro*.

Mozart (seated) with his father Leopold and sister Nannerl

High and low notes

How high or low an instrument can play depends on its size and length. Wind instruments (instruments that you blow) play high or low notes depending on the length of the tube they are made from. Large wind instruments can play lower notes than smaller wind instruments.

High and low notes on the clarinet

When you play the lowest note on the clarinet (low E), you are covering all the holes. To play higher notes, you have to uncover some of the holes. When you do this, you shorten the tube because you allow air to escape before it reaches the bottom. The more holes you uncover, the shorter the tube gets, so the higher the note is.

Soldier's march

Schumann wrote this march for his *Album for the Young*. Try to make a big difference between the *forte* and *piano* sections, and play the notes as short as possible where they are marked staccato.

Dotted quavers

A dotted quaver and semiquaver

A dotted quaver lasts for one and a half quaver beats, or three semiquaver beats.

Waltz

This tune was written by a Polish composer called Fryderyk Chopin (1810-1849). A waltz is a lively, swirling dance with three beats in each bar. Waltzes became very popular in the 19th century.

Dancing a waltz

Moderato

Playing higher notes

To play higher notes, you press a key at the back of the clarinet with your left-hand thumb. It is called the speaker key. When you press it, it allows air to escape from the top joint. This is like making the tube shorter, so the notes get higher.

Make sure your thumb still covers the back thumb hole when you press the speaker key or you will probably hear a squeak. You also need to tighten your lips a little. You may have to blow a bit harder for these notes, but don't blow too hard or the sound might be harsh.

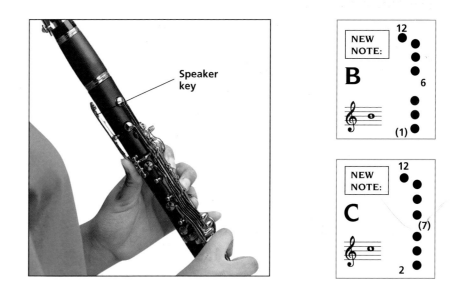

Sumer is icumen in

This 13th century song is a type of piece called a canon. In a canon, several people play the same tune, but starting a few bars apart. You could try playing this piece with some friends. When the first person reaches the number 2, the second player starts playing from the beginning. When the first person reaches the number 3, the third player starts from the beginning, and so on.

If you want to play the canon on your own, try recording the tune on a tape. Then play back the recording and join in.

Section of an early manuscript of the beginning of *Sumer is icumen in*

Playing above B flat

As you move from lower notes to higher notes, you take your fingers off the clarinet one by one. When you reach B flat, you are only using two fingers. But to play the B natural or the C above this note, you need to put all your fingers back on the holes. This can be fairly tricky, so you may need to practise until you can do it smoothly.

Try the exercise below a few times, slowly at first, then gradually getting faster. It will help if you keep your fingers close to the holes, as in the picture, so you can put them down quickly when you need to.

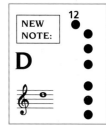

NEW NOTE:
D

Pretty Polly Oliver

Pastoral symphony

A symphony is a piece for an orchestra in several sections, called movements. This tune is from a symphony by Beethoven. *Legato* means "smoothly".

Pause marks

The sign on the left is a pause mark. It tells you to make the note last a little bit longer than usual.

NEW NOTE: 12

E

From the New World

From the New World is a symphony by Antonín Dvořák (1841-1904) a Czech composer. It was written in America. At that time, many people thought of America as the "new world". The symphony was first performed at Carnegie Hall in New York. *Largo* means "very slowly". *Rit.* is short for *ritardando*. It means "get gradually slower". The last note has a pause mark over it, so hold it for a bit longer than four crotchet beats.

Carnegie Hall

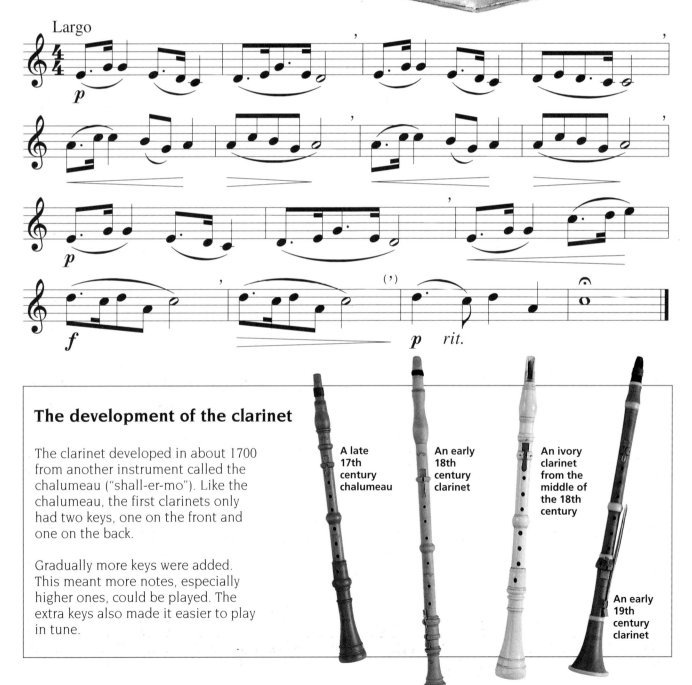

The development of the clarinet

The clarinet developed in about 1700 from another instrument called the chalumeau ("shall-er-mo"). Like the chalumeau, the first clarinets only had two keys, one on the front and one on the back.

Gradually more keys were added. This meant more notes, especially higher ones, could be played. The extra keys also made it easier to play in tune.

A late 17th century chalumeau

An early 18th century clarinet

An ivory clarinet from the middle of the 18th century

An early 19th century clarinet

Scarborough fair

Triplets

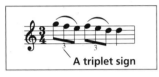

A triplet sign tells you to play three quavers in the time of two. There are three triplet quavers in one crotchet beat. On the left you can see two groups of triplets followed by a crotchet.

Scheherazade

This music is by a Russian composer called Nikolay Rimsky-Korsakov (1844-1908). The rhythm may seem a bit tricky at first, so make sure you count very carefully. A *tempo* means return to the original speed after getting slower at the *rit*.

Title page of the music for Scheherazade

27

3/2 time

 This time signature means there are three minim beats in each bar.

Dotted semibreves

 A dotted semibreve lasts for six crotchet beats.

Alla danza

This tune is from a piece called the *Water Music Suite*, by Goerge Frideric Handel (1685-1759). It was composed for King George I of England in the early 18th century, for a royal outing on the River Thames. *ff* stands for *fortissimo*, which means "very loud".

George I's royal outing on the River Thames

The Boehm system

Theobald Boehm was a German flute player. He invented a new key system for the flute which improved the tuning. Boehm's flutes were also louder and easier to play. In the mid-1800s, Boehm's idea was applied to the clarinet. The new design was very popular and is still used today.

A modern clarinet with Boehm's key system

Clarinet concerto

A concerto is a piece of music written for an orchestra, with a special part for a solo instrument. This tune is from a concerto by Mozart in which the solo instrument is the clarinet. The clarinet was one of Mozart's favourite instruments. He wrote this concerto for his friend Anton Stadler, a famous clarinettist. This tune is from the second movement.

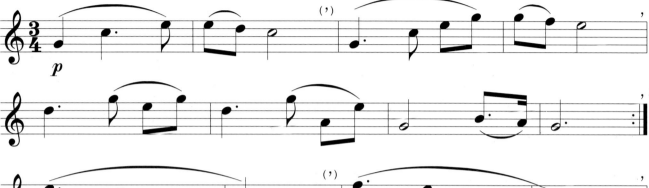

A clarinet from Mozart's time

Lullaby

This tune is by Johannes Brahms (1833-1897), a German composer and pianist who was born in Hamburg (shown right). It is one of his most famous compositions. *Cantabile* means "in a singing style".

NEW NOTE:	12
F♯	

Andante cantabile

29

Greensleeves

This English tune was written in the 16th century. At this time, people often gathered together to sing and play music with their friends. On the right you can see some 16th century musicians singing and playing instruments. Some people believe this tune was written by King Henry VIII of England, though this is unlikely.

NEW NOTE: **G♯** 10

Serenade

Originally a serenade was a love song, played out of doors. Later it became a popular style of instrumental music. Usually serenades were played in the evening. This one is by Haydn.

NEW NOTE: **A** 12

Spring

The pieces on this page are both from a set of four concertos called *The Four Seasons*, written by an Italian composer called Antonio Vivaldi (1678-1741). Each concerto is based on a poem.

Trill signs

The sign on the left tells you to play a trill. To do this, you alternate very quickly between the note that is written and the note above it. Make sure you keep the rhythm steady.

Winter

Tenuto marks

A short line above or below a note is called a tenuto mark. It tells you to hold the note for its full time value or even a little longer.

NEW NOTE:

C♯

Toreador's song

This tune is from an opera called *Carmen* by Georges Bizet (1838-1875). An opera is a play set to music. A toreador is a bullfighter.

Emperor quartet

A quartet is a piece for four instruments, each playing a separate line of music. This tune is from a quartet by Haydn for two violins, a viola and a cello. It is now also the German national anthem.

A string quartet

A different way to play C sharp

Sometimes you need to use different fingerings for some notes. In the third line of *Minuet* below, there is a C sharp straight after a C. It is almost impossible to play this smoothly if you use the fingering for C sharp on page 32, because you have to move the little finger of your right hand across the keys too quickly. Instead, play C sharp with a left-hand key, using the fingering on the right.

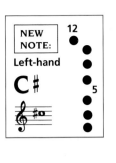

Minuet

These two tunes are from a piece by Mozart called *Eine kleine Nachtmusik* ("A little night music"). A minuet is an elegant dance with three beats in a bar.

Dancing a minuet

Romance

The picture on the right shows the manuscript for *Eine kleine Nachtmusik* in Mozart's own handwriting. This music was originally written for a group of four or five stringed instruments. Today it is one of his most famous pieces.

D.S. *al Fine*

D.S. *al Fine* tells you to go back to the sign 𝄋 , play the music again until you reach the word *Fine*, then stop.

Playing A sharp

A sharp (shown on the right) is another name for B flat. Play it with the same fingering you use for B flat.

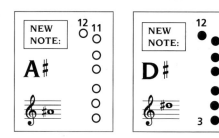

Mexican hat dance

The time signature changes in this piece. Keep the quavers the same speed throughout, but count in groups of three for 6/8 and groups of two for 3/4.

Fine

D.S. al Fine

Yellow bird

This tune is from Haiti, an island in the Caribbean Sea. The rhythm in the last two lines may seem a little tricky at first. Practise clapping these bars before you play the whole piece. Make sure you count the tied notes carefully.

A Caribbean steel band

Basse danse

The basse danse was very popular during the 15th and 16th centuries. It was often danced at social occasions. Instead of lifting their feet, the dancers pushed them across the floor in slow, smooth movements.

Long pointed shoes meant dancers had to tread carefully during the basse danse.

Transposing instruments

Unlike modern clarinets, the earliest models only played a few notes. To play music with more notes, players needed three instruments of different lengths, each of which played at a different pitch. To make it easier for players to change from one type of clarinet to another, each written note was played with the same fingering on each instrument. But for a written C, one sounded a C, one sounded a B flat and one sounded an A.

Instruments which sound at a different pitch from the written music are called transposing instruments. The standard clarinet model used today is known as the clarinet in B flat. This means that when you play a written C, you hear a B flat. On a clarinet in A, a written C sounds as an A. Below you can see some other examples of transposing instruments, as well as some that do not transpose.

The trumpet (above) is in B flat, like the standard clarinet used today.

Most stringed instruments, such as the violin (below), do not transpose.

The alto saxophone is in E flat, so the written note C sounds as E flat.

The flute (below) is not a transposing instrument.

D.C. *al Fine*

D.C. *al Fine* stands for *Da Capo al Fine*. This tells you to go back to the beginning and play the music again until you reach the word *Fine*. Then you stop.

Tambourin

A tambourin is a French folk dance. Tambourins were often accompanied by a pipe and a tabor (a type of drum). You can see some people dancing a tambourin with a pipe and tabor player on the right.

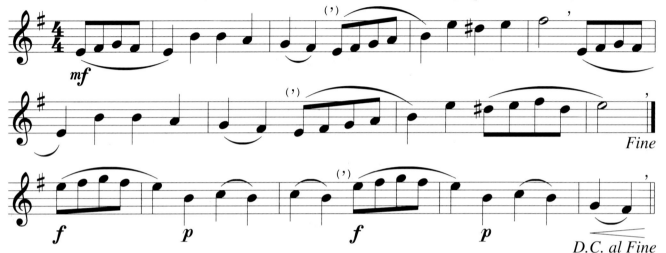

D.C. al Fine

Aylesford's piece

This tune is by Handel. In this piece you need to play C with a left-hand key (number 7) where it follows E flat.

Playing E flat

E flat (shown on the right) is another name for D sharp. Play it with the same fingering as you use for D sharp.

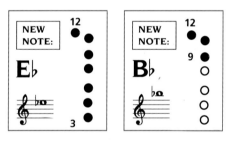

Minuet in D minor

This tune (along with *Minuet in* G on page 18) is from a set of keyboard pieces by Bach. He wrote them for his wife Anna Magdalena. On the right you can see Bach's inscription to his wife at the beginning of his keyboard book.

Modern clarinets

In the 19th century, when Boehm's key system was adapted to the clarinet (see page 28), the range of notes that could be played increased. This meant that players had to change instruments less frequently (see page 35). The B flat clarinet gradually became the most popular, because people believed it had the best tone. It is still the most common type today, though the clarinet in A is still often used in orchestras.

Other instruments in the family include the high-pitched E flat clarinet, the alto and bass clarinets (which are lower in pitch) and the contrabass clarinet. The contrabass has the lowest pitch and is almost 3m (9ft) long. You have to rest it on the floor to play it. These instruments are usually used in wind bands and orchestras, rather than for solo playing.

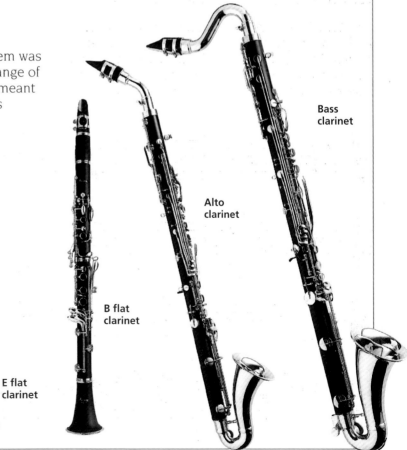

E flat clarinet

B flat clarinet

Alto clarinet

Bass clarinet

Drinking song

This tune is from an opera called *La Traviata*, by Verdi (1813-1901). In the picture on the right you can see a costume made for a performance of the opera.

A scene from *La Traviata*

The college hornpipe

A hornpipe is a very lively dance with four beats in each bar.

Sailors dancing a hornpipe

D.S. al Fine

Danse des mirlitons

This tune is from a ballet called *The Nutcracker*, by the Russian composer Pyotr Il'yich Tchaikovsky (1840-1893).

Grace notes

Grace note

A grace note is an extra note used to decorate the music. Play it very quickly, just before the next beat.

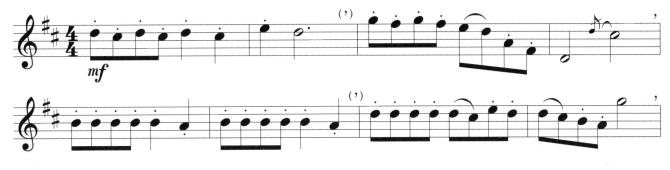

Clarinets from around the world

Many different types of clarinet are played around the world. You can see some of them here.

This Indian pipe is made from bone, rope and an animal horn.

This Spanish clarinet has two cane pipes with an animal horn at each end.

This is a double clarinet from Central Europe. It has two reeds and two pipes.

This double clarinet from Brazil is as tall as a human being. The reeds are inside the pipes, so you cannot see them.

The South American clarinet on the left is made from a dried fruit shell called a gourd. The shell is attached to a piece of cane. There is a single reed inside the top of the piece of cane.

This West African clarinet is made from cane and dried fruit shells. The reed is on one side of the cane. There are holes in each shell to alter the pitch.

Playing duets

Duets are pieces for two people. Each person plays a
different part. The parts for the next three duets are
printed on opposite pages. Before playing a duet,
check that your clarinets are in tune with each other
by playing a B together. You can make the pitch of
your clarinet lower by pulling the barrel out a little.

Moving on up

Banana boat song

Moving on up (duet part)

This piece is in a style known as jazz. The rhythm is a bit tricky, so learn your own part before playing it as a duet. Then decide how fast to play and count a bar out loud before you start. Play steadily and don't stop if you make a mistake. It can help to learn both parts and swap them over.

A jazz band

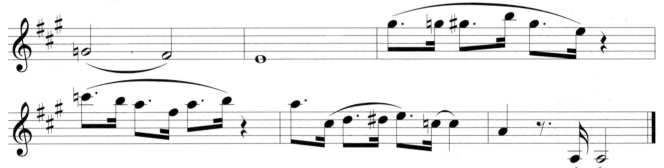

Banana boat song (duet part)

Prelude in D minor

This piece is by J.S. Bach. Bach's father was a musician and three of his sons became composers. Play the music below by yourself, or ask a friend to play the music on page 43 with you as a duet.

The Bach family playing music together

Prelude in D minor (duet part)

On the right you can see the town of Leipzig, in Germany, where Bach lived and worked for most of his life. He was the director of St. Thomas' Church there from 1723 until he died in 1750.

The three kings

You can play the tunes on these two pages on your own or with a piano. Before you try them with a piano, practise your own part separately. Then make sure you are in tune with the piano. Because the clarinet is a transposing instrument (see page 35), your B should sound the same as an A on the piano. Count carefully and keep a steady beat. This tune is by Peter Cornelius (1824-1874).

Narcissus

The story of Narcissus comes from ancient Greece. Narcissus was a very handsome man and many women loved him. But he thought he was too good for them. One day he saw his reflection in a pool of water and decided that the only person he could fall in love with was himself. He was so heartbroken when he realized this that he died. This tune is by Ethelbert Nevin (1862-1901).

Music help

The list below explains the Italian words used in this book. The words in **bold** tell you how to pronounce them. Read the pronunciation words exactly as they are written.

andante	**an-dan-tay**	at a walking pace, a bit slower than *moderato*
allegretto	**a-luh-gretto**	fairly lively, not as fast as *allegro*
allegro	**a-leg-ro**	fast and lively
a tempo	**ah tempo**	at the original speed
cantabile	**cant-ah-be-lay**	in a singing style
crescendo (*cresc.*)	**cruh-shen-doh**	getting louder
D.C. *al Fine*	**dee cee al fee-nay**	repeat from the beginning to the *Fine* sign
diminuendo (*dim.*)	**dim-in-you-en-doh**	getting quieter
Fine	**fee-nay**	stop
forte (*f*)	**for-tay**	loud
fortissimo (*ff*)	**for-tiss-im-oh**	very loud
largo	**lar-go**	very slow
legato	**leg-ah-toe**	smoothly
mezzo forte (*mf*)	**met-so for-tay**	fairly loud
mezzo piano (*mp*)	**met-so pee-ah-no**	fairly quiet
moderato	**mod-er-ah-toe**	at a moderate speed
pianissimo (*pp*)	**pee-an-iss-im-oh**	very quiet
piano (*p*)	**pee-ah-no**	quiet
ritardando (*rit.*)	**rit-ar-dan-doh**	getting slower
staccato	**stack-ah-toe**	detached, short

Fingering chart

This chart shows the fingering for all the notes in this book. The fingering diagrams are explained on page 3. You can find out about fingerings with numbers in brackets on pages 16 and 17.

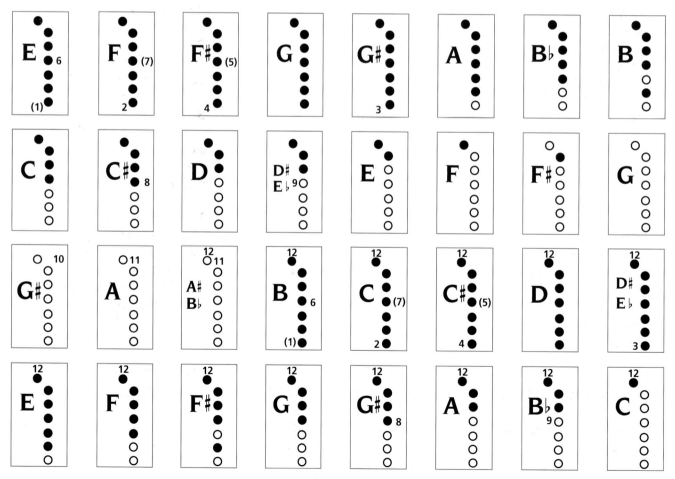

46

Clarinet music to listen to

Below are some suggestions for clarinet music you could try listening to.

Arnold	Concerto	**Mendelssohn**	Konzertstück in D minor
	Sonatina	**Milhaud**	Duo Concertant
Banks	Night Piece	**Mozart**	Concerto
	Blues for two		Divertimento no.2
Bilk	Stranger on the Shore	**Nielsen**	Concerto
Brahms	Sonata no.1	**Patterson**	Conversations
	Sonata no.2	**Poulenc**	Sonata
A. Cooke	Concerto	**Reger**	Romanze
	Sonata	**Rimsky-Korsakov**	Concerto for military band
Crusell	Concerto	**Rossini**	Theme and variations
	Quartet in C minor	**Schumann**	Fantasiestücke
Debussy	Première Rhapsodie	**Seiber**	Andantino Pastorale
Ferguson	Four Short Pieces	**Spohr**	Concertos
Finzi	Five Bagatelles	**C. Stamitz**	Concerto no.3
	Concerto	**J. Stamitz**	Concerto
Gershwin	Rhapsody in Blue	**C. Stanford**	Sonata
Hindemith	Sonata	**Stravinsky**	Trois Pièces
Ireland	Fantasy Sonata		Ebony Concerto
Lefèvre	Sonatas	**Weber**	Grand Duo Concertant
Lutoslawski	Dance Preludes		Theme and variations
Maxwell Davies	Hymnos		Concertino
	The Seven Brightnesses		Concertos

Index of tunes

Index

Acknowledgements

The publishers would like to thank Christopher Hampson,
Steven Hunte and Lorraine Morgon who were
photographed for this book; also Bill Lewington Musical
Instruments, London, for supplying the instruments in
the photographs. The photograph of the18th century
ivory clarinet on page 26 is reproduced by kind
permission of the Royal College of Music, London.
Thanks also go to Ackerman and Reynolds, East Sussex,
for supplying the other early clarinets photographed on
page 26.

First published in 1995 by Usborne Publishing Ltd,
Usborne House, 83-85 Saffron Hill, London EC1N 8RT.

Printed in Portugal.